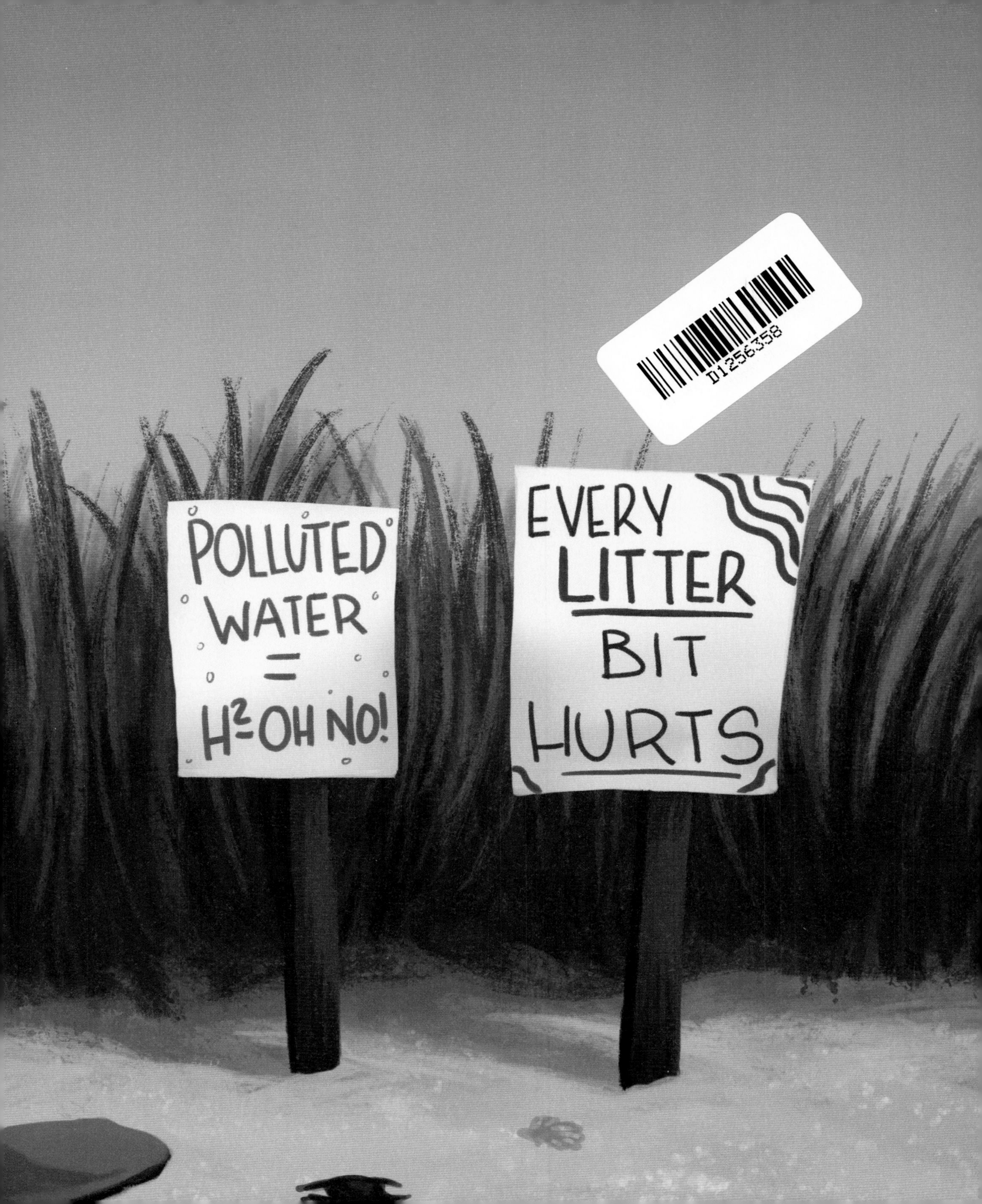
POLLUTED WATER
=
H^2OH NO!
EVERY LITTER BIT HURTS

To Don:
Thank you for always being by my side on all my
adventures. You are truly the best. I love you.

To my little inspirations, Sarafina and Lucia:
Your imaginations took me on a magical journey
where dreams really do become a reality.
Thank you, my loves.

Laura Mancuso

To Mom, Dad, and Brother:

Thank you for your unwavering support;

I would not be where I am without it.

To Sara:

Finding animals in the pool has never been the same.

Jenna Guidi

www.mascotbooks.com

The Fin-Tastic Cleanup

For more information, please contact:
Mascot Books
620 Herndon Parkway, Suite 320
Herndon, VA 20170
info@mascotbooks.com

Library of Congress Control Number: 2020913268

CPSIA Code: PRT1120A
ISBN-13: 978-1-64543-671-3

Printed in the United States

Thank you for your Support! Make a Splash! ♡ Laura Guidi

The Fin-Tastic Cleanup

Laura Mancuso

Illustrated by Jenna Guidi

It was a beautiful Monday morning.
Three little mermaids zipped through their city without warning.
They were dressed in their favorite shells, pearls, and frocks,
playfully ducking behind coral, plants, and rocks.

Their names were Sara, Alix, and Lucy.
They lived under the deep blue sea.
They decorated their cottages with pretty shells and such.
The mermaids loved their homes so much.

As they headed to the beach, they passed their buddy, who complained of a sore.
Finn the fish said he hurt himself on something he'd never seen before.

It was a cracked plastic bottle half buried in the sand,
with a sharp part sticking out.
Finn said, "That's it! I swam by that, hit my fin, and began to shout!"

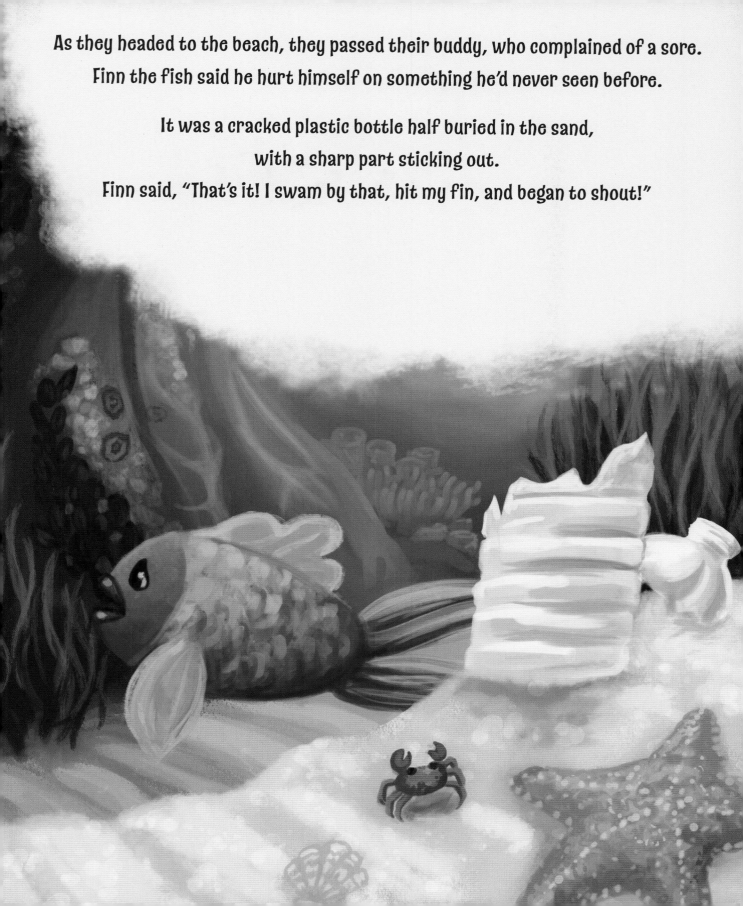

Alix explained, "Wrap it in kelp. It may sting, so try not to yelp."

Finn replied, "It already feels better. Thank you, mer-ladies, for all your help."

Lucy took the bottle out of the sand.

She swam it to the surface and left it on land.

Sara looked worried and said,
"I hope that doesn't make it down here again."
Alix agreed, "Trash doesn't belong here; it's not very zen."

The mermaids decided to head back to town.
Once again, they spotted a friend with a frown.
They stopped Sally the seal to see what could be wrong.
Sally shared her story as they swam along.

Sally explained that she was looking for lunch.
She scooped up something colorful, and began to munch.
Turned out it wasn't food; it was a plastic bag!
Within seconds, Sally started to gag!

Thank goodness for her pal, Doris the duck.
She helped Sally cough that bag up; it landed right in the muck.

Sara dug the bag out of the muck and shouted, "That's enough!
We need a plan to get rid of this trash, but it's going to be tough."

Sara swam toward the surface, but on her way up,
she nearly choked on an old fishing lure.
Now Sara was upset; she didn't want her home and friends harmed anymore.

When Sara reached the beach, she was gasping for breath.
Shortly after, she was greeted by a young girl named Beth.

"Hi, my friends and I are cleaning up the coast."
Beth continued, "We are nature lovers, but we love the beach the most."

Looking at Beth and her friends, Sara suddenly came up with a brilliant plan.
Sara asked, "Would your mates help us get this trash into a garbage can?"
The three little mermaids would grab the garbage from the sea.
Sara then explained, "We'd swim it ashore to where you would be,
and your crew can collect it from us and dispose of it properly."

Beth and her friends agreed, and the girls sprang to work immediately.

Sara, Alix, and Lucy split up and covered each part of their city.
They saved sea animals entangled in debris.
After a week of collecting trash, the mermaids had over one hundred bins!
They brought them to the surface with the help of some extra fins.

Beth and her friends were ready and waiting.
They took all the garbage that needed eliminating.
The two teams cheered and began to chatter.
The mermaids and humans knew constant cleanup was an important matter.

"Hey," said the mermaids, "Let's meet all the time!
We can keep the ocean clean and in its prime."

Beth turned to the mermaids and said, "This leaves us with a difficult question...
one that welcomes any suggestion.
We are just one dedicated club at one beach.
How can we clean litter when it's far out of reach?"

Lucy turned to her friends and said, "Together, we can create a solution.
Our planet should be free from this endless pollution."

33rd Annual International Coastal Cleanup of the
Ocean Conservancy Organization 2019 Report:

1,080,358 volunteers in a worldwide effort of 122 countries walked over 22,000 miles of coastline. These volunteers removed 23,333,816 pounds of garbage from our oceans and recorded their findings on Clean Swell or printed data forms.

The Ocean Conservancy Organization

Top 10 of Debris items found in oceans:

1) Cigarette butts: 5,716,331
2) Food wrappers: 3,728,712
3) Straws/stirrers: 3,668,871
4) Forks, knives, spoons: 1,968,065
5) Plastic beverage bottles: 1,754,908
6) Plastic bottle caps: 1,390,232
7) Plastic grocery bags: 964,541
8) Other plastic bags: 938,929
9) Plastic lids: 728,892
10) Plastic cups, plates: 656,276

Approximately 1.4 billion pounds of trash per year enters the ocean.
National Oceanic Atmospheric Administration

Worldwide, 13,000 to 15,000 pieces of plastic are dumped into the ocean every day.
Ocean Crusaders

It can take 20 to 100 years for a plastic bag to break up. Plastic bags never fully break down; they just break into smaller pieces causing animals to mistake it for food and creating a toxic effect on our water.
Ocean Crusaders

Approximately 1 million sea birds and 100,000 sea mammals are killed a year due to pollution.
Ocean Crusaders

Names of environmental groups you can join nationally and locally:

National Oceanic Atmospheric Administration (NOAA) *www.noaa.gov*

Ocean Conservancy Organization *www.oceanconservancy.org*

Ocean Crusaders *www.oceancrusaders.com*

The Blue Frontier campaign *www.bluefront.org*

Greenpeace *www.greenpeace.org*

4ocean *www.4ocean.com*

Surfrider Foundation *www.surfrider.org*

NY Marine Rescue Center *www.nymarinerescue.org*

Atlantic Marine Conservation Society *www.amseas.org*

Cooperative Extension Suffolk County *www.ccesuffolk.org/marine*

About the Author

Laura Mancuso grew up loving the beach and marine biology in St. James, New York. After graduating from the University of Buffalo, she continued to live and work in Buffalo with her husband. However, she missed the ocean, her friends, and her family, so she moved back to Long Island. Inspired by her daughters, Laura decided to start writing children's books. She wanted to bring joy to reading for young kids, but hoped to draw awareness to our waters and what we can do to preserve them. This is Laura's first book. She currently resides in Hampton Bays, where you can find her with her family at one of its many beautiful beaches.

About the Illustrator

Jenna Guidi grew up on Long Island and studied
illustration and animation at the School of Visual Arts
in New York City. She has loved Disney and Pixar films
since she was young, which sparked her lifelong interest
in art. When she is not drawing, she is usually reading,
baking, and drinking tea. Traveling has given her a greater
appreciation of the earth, and she believes we must do the
best we can to take care of our planet and each other.

DON'T SINK THE DRINK
We are GREEN & We are CLEAN
-THINK- BLUE, -GO- GREEN